AF541308

Three selected fables from three different countries of the world

An imprint of Om Books International

Published in 2012 by

OM KIDZ

An imprint of Om Books International

Corporate & Editorial Office
A 12, Sector 64, Noida 201 301
Uttar Pradesh, India
Phone: +91 120 477 4100
Email: editorial@ombooks.com
Website: www.ombooksinternational.com

Sales Office
4379/4B, Prakash House, Ansari Road
Darya Ganj, New Delhi 110 002, India
Phone: +91 11 2326 3363, 2326 5303
Fax: +91 11 2327 8091
Email: sales@ombooks.com
Website: www.ombooks.com

Research and Content: Anirban Sarkar, Bidisha Roychoudhury
Design and Illustration: Partha Pratim Das, Nilmoni Raha

ISBN: 978-93-80070-71-1

Printed in China

10 9 8 7 6 5 4 3 2 1

Contents

OLD INDIAN FABLE

THE BLUE JACKAL

Many years ago there lived a jackal in a forest in India. He was known as Chandaraka. One day, Chandaraka felt very hungry. But he could not find any food in the forest. So he thought, "Let me go to the nearby village and steal some food from the people living there."

He went to a small village at the end of the forest. He was starving since morning and tried to break into the very first house that came his way.

Unfortunately, as he was just about to enter the house, a group of dogs spotted him. The moment they saw the jackal trying to sneak into the house, they started to bark at the top of their voices.

"Hey, you sly old jackal, you can't get away, trying to steal food from that house. We will teach you a lesson!"

This scared the jackal to no limit. He ran as fast as he could. He took a left turn and a right turn, ran amok through the alleyways and the squares and the parks. Finally, he rushed into a washer man's house.

While trying to hide, the jackal slipped and fell into a tub full of blue colour. It was a tub where the washer man had mixed indigo in water to dye the clothes.

The dogs could not find Chandaraka and gave up. Their barks soon faded into silence.

When the dogs stopped barking and went away, he pulled himself out of the tub.

There was a big mirror fixed on the wall of the house. As soon as the jackal saw himself in the mirror he exclaimed: "O my God, what happened to my beautiful slender body? It's all blue now!"

When Chandaraka reached the forest, every animal failed to recognise him. “Run, run, run! A horrible beast has entered our forest,” said the tiger. “Or maybe the Devil himself! He will eat us up. Run, run, run,” cried the elephant.

They began to run towards other corners of the forest.

At this point, the jackal hit upon a plan. “Let me take advantage of the situation.” He asked, “Why are you running like this? Do not fear. I am not the Devil. I am sent by God. He told me that animals in this forest do not have a ruler. So they have become very unruly. God has sent me here as your king. If you obey me, there is nothing to fear.”

The innocent animals believed the shrewd jackal and accepted him as their king.

The jackal appointed different animals in different positions. Chandaraka pointed to a lion and said, “Lion, you are brave and fast. You shall be my minister.” This made the tiger unhappy. Seeing that, the jackal said, “Tiger, don’t be sad. You shall be my chamberlain.” He asked the wolf to be the gatekeeper.

One fine evening, Chandaraka was holding his court. A small messy duckling was caught while stealing worms from another duck's area. Chandaraka was listening to the charges with a royal frown. He looked very serious.

When the blue jackal was busy with the trial of the duckling, a pack of jackals were passing by. They were howling and singing to celebrate the bright moonlit night.

Just as the jackal heard their call, he forgot for a moment about the trick he was playing. And he joined the chorus!

“Dear friends, he is just an ordinary jackal!” said the lion. “A blue-coloured jackal, not any king!” roared the tiger. “Catch him, thrash him, kill him now!” said the duckling as she stretched her wings.

Until then the duckling was trembling with fear, waiting for the king’s verdict. But as soon as they found out the jackal’s tricks the fear melted in the air. She felt excited, she felt important. She flapped her wings and stretched her legs. Then yawned a bit as she missed her siesta and had to come for the trial.

Being exposed, the jackal tried to flee. But the big fat bear grabbed Chandaraka by the neck and threw him at the angry crowd.

All the animals pounced on the jackal and killed him right away.

FABULOUS FACT

The ancient Egyptians used to worship a jackal-headed God.

OLD AMERICAN FABLE

KAREYA AND THE COYOTE

Many hundred snows ago, Kareya, the old American God, created the world.

First, He made big water bodies where He released different types of fishes. He made trees on land and animals to roam about. Then He thought, “There must be something for the air too.” He began to create all the big and small birds one after another. “O, these birds are so beautiful!” Kareya praised His own creation as He looked at the birds, bright and gay, tweeting all the way. “I must make some birds for land too.” Thus, He made hens and ducks, penguins and ostriches.

Finally, He decided to create a man. He filled the man's head with some grey pulp. The man called it 'brain'.

At that time, all the animals were equally powerful. Kareya thought, "There has to be a division of rank according to their strength." He asked all the animals to gather at a certain place. One by one, they started to come to Him.

When Kareya saw all the animals in front of Him, He said to the man, "I have made you the wisest of all. Make bows and arrows of different sizes and give them to all the animals, one by one, to set the order of their power. The animal who receives the biggest bow and arrow will become the most powerful of all. The smallest bow and arrow will go to the weakest. You have to decide who deserves to be the most powerful and who the least."

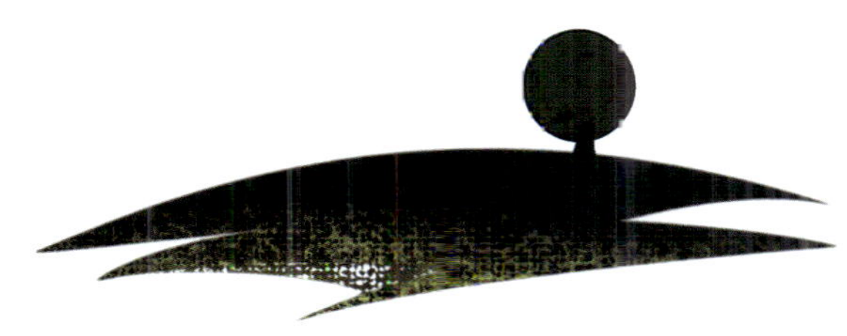

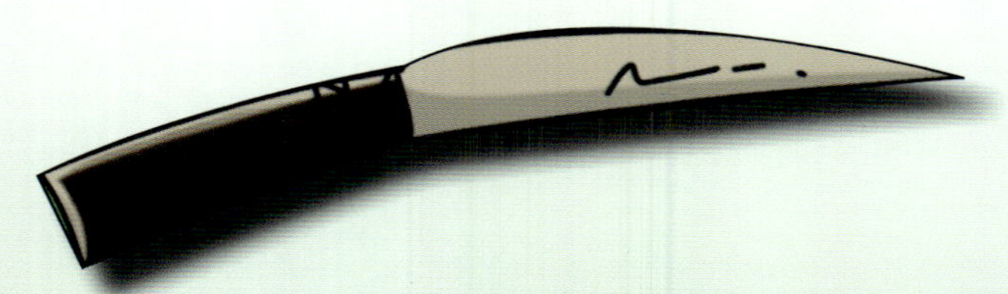

The man did as he was told. He took nine nights and nine days to complete the task.

On the ninth night, all the animals went to sleep early. Nobody wanted to be late at the next day's meeting. The next morning they would meet the man to find out who would become more powerful than whom. They were very excited. And anxious too. All went to sleep with butterflies in their stomach.

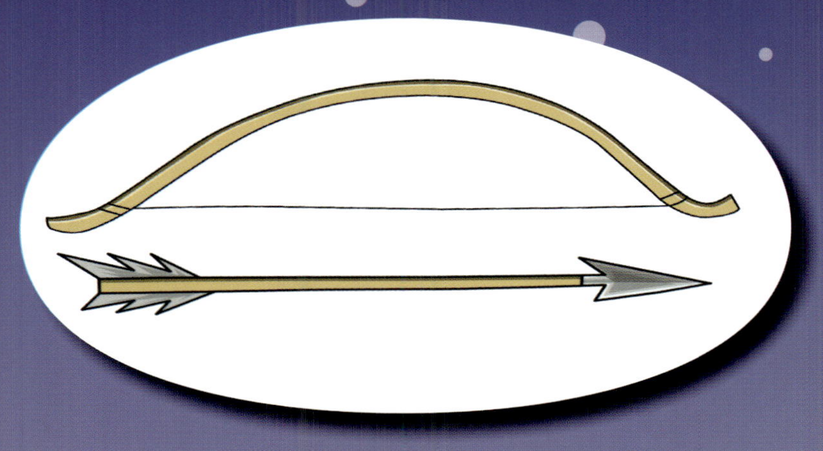

That night, the coyote did not go to sleep. “If I can stay awake and reach the man before anyone else, I would get the biggest bow and arrow and would become the most powerful of all. Then I will be able to eat up all the other animals,” he lisped as he came up with his wicked plan.

However, about midnight, he began to feel sleepy. He walked about the camp and rubbed his eyes several times. He then started jumping about to stay awake all night. All of this worked for sometime, but slowly he grew tired and started feeling sleepy again.

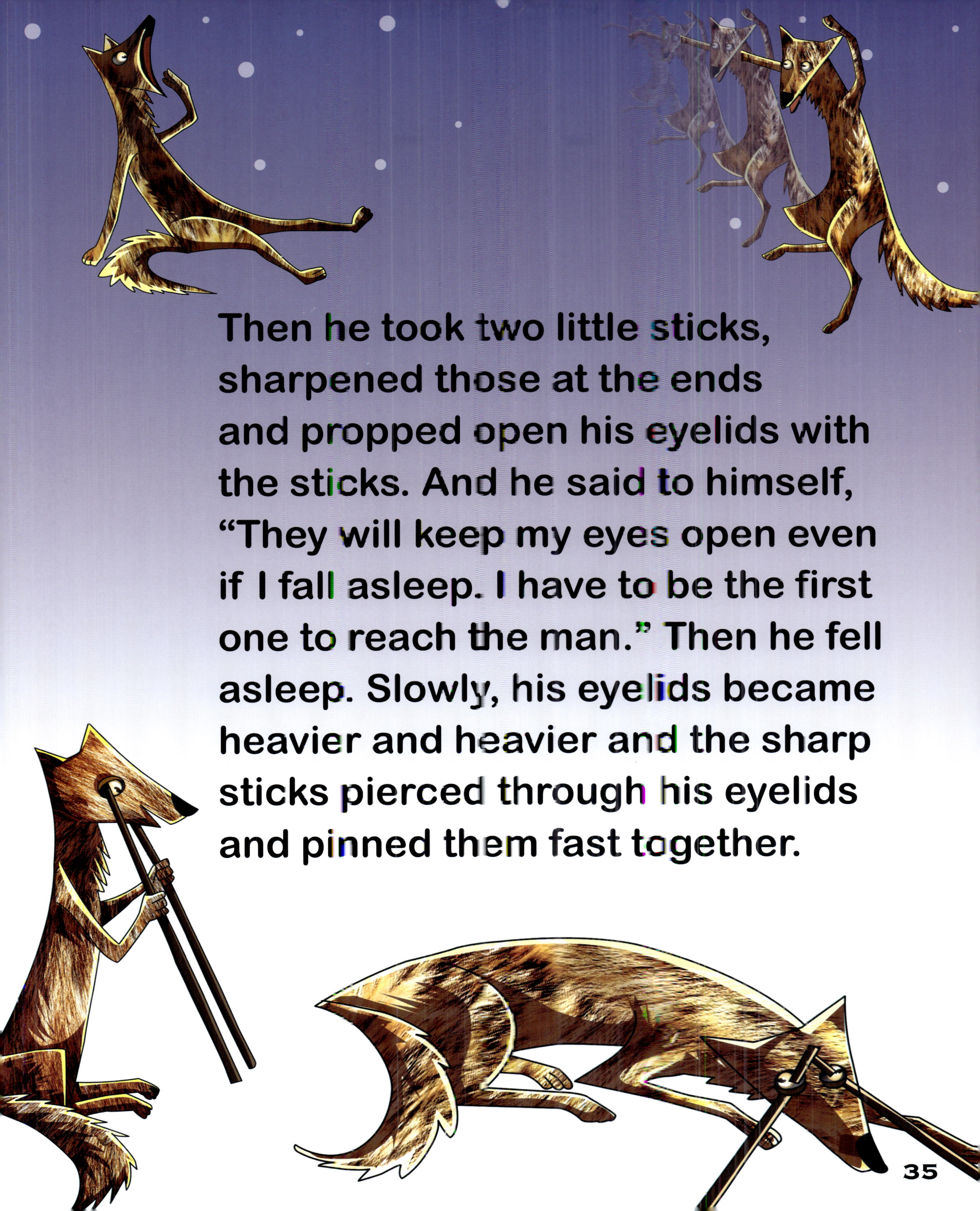

Then he took two little sticks, sharpened those at the ends and propped open his eyelids with the sticks. And he said to himself, “They will keep my eyes open even if I fall asleep. I have to be the first one to reach the man.” Then he fell asleep. Slowly, his eyelids became heavier and heavier and the sharp sticks pierced through his eyelids and pinned them fast together.

All the animals woke up early next morning and rustled up for the meeting.

They gathered round the man. They were very curious and excited. The man started to give out the bows and arrows one by one.

The tiger got the biggest one. "Ahhhh! I am the most powerful!"

He was very happy and started to jump. The bear came second. The poor frog got the smallest bow and a very short needle-like arrow. "I thought you would give me the biggest one because I am small in size and need more power," he complained, but all in vain.

There was still one bow and one arrow left with the man. “Who did I miss out?” he wondered.

He went looking for the last animal and found the coyote still sleeping. The man woke him up, took the sticks out of his eyelids and gave him the last and smallest bow and arrow.

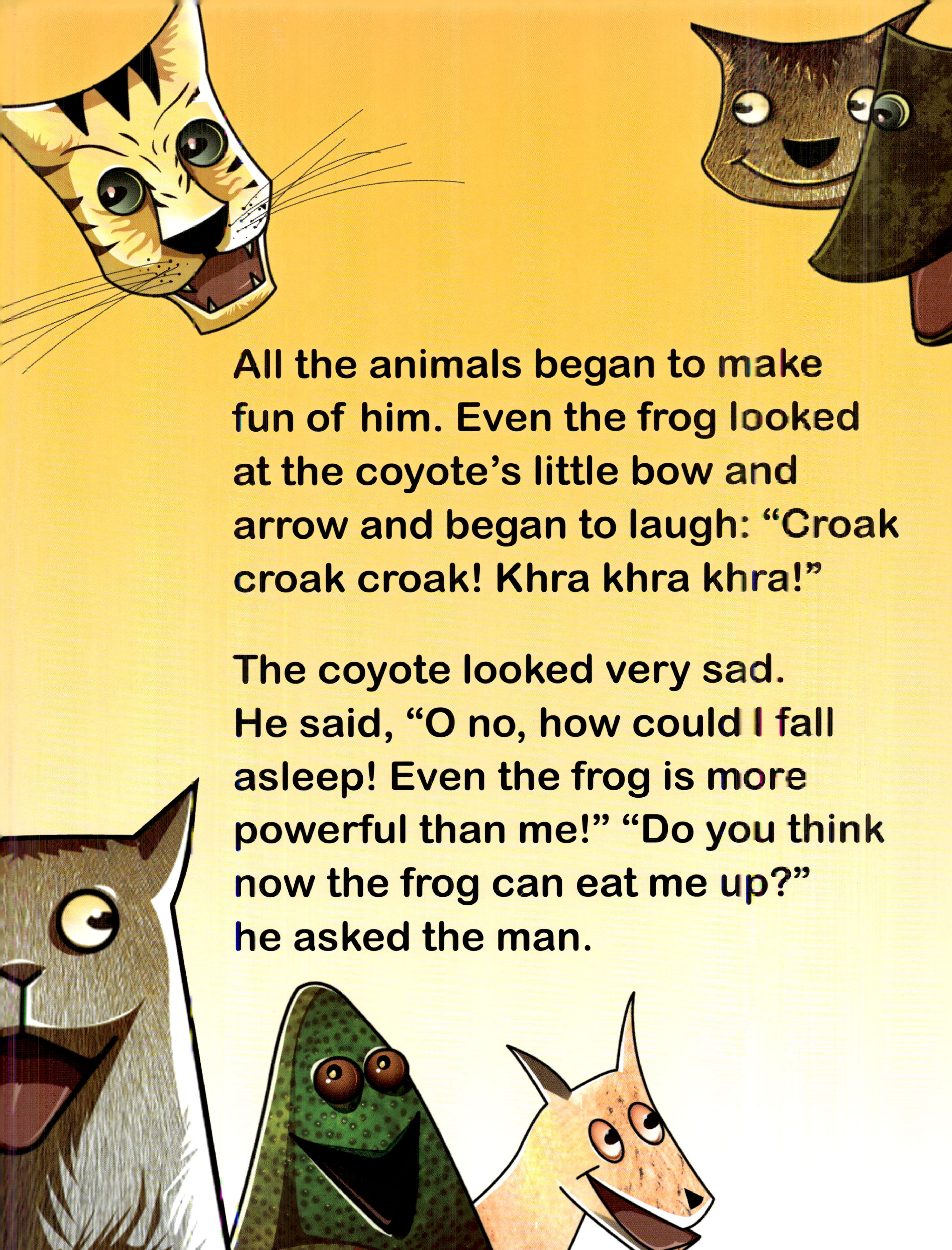

All the animals began to make fun of him. Even the frog looked at the coyote's little bow and arrow and began to laugh: "Croak croak croak! Khra khra khra!"

The coyote looked very sad. He said, "O no, how could I fall asleep! Even the frog is more powerful than me!" "Do you think now the frog can eat me up?" he asked the man.

The man took pity on the coyote and prayed to Kareya for him. The man said, “O dear Kareya, please help this poor creature. Please do something about him. Or else, being the weakest, he won’t be able to live.”

At first He said, “Serves him right. He tried to be too smart. It’s all his fault.” However, Kareya was a kind God. As He looked at the sad and sobbing coyote, He changed His mind. He thought for a while and then He said, “Though the coyote is the weakest, he will be the most cunning animal. He will also live among human beings.”

Thus, the coyote became the most cunning of all animals. And coyotes still live near villages and big cities where humans live.

FABULOUS FACT

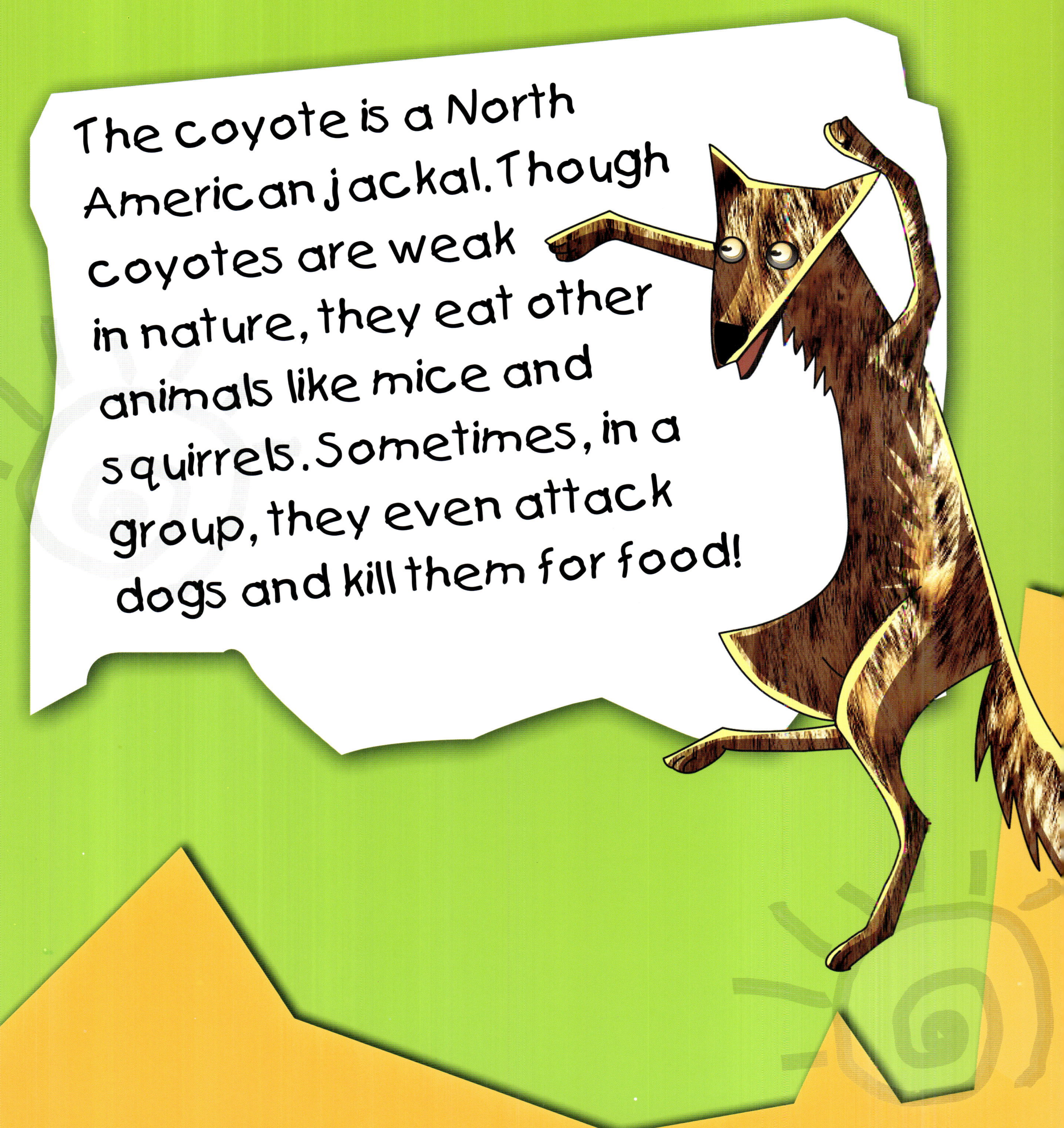

The coyote is a North American jackal. Though coyotes are weak in nature, they eat other animals like mice and squirrels. Sometimes, in a group, they even attack dogs and kill them for food!

OLD CHINESE FABLE

THE CHINESE TIGER AND THE INDIAN DONKEY

There was a time when nobody had seen donkeys in the land of Guizhou in China. A businessman from Guizhou went to India to buy spices. He saw a strange animal grazing in a meadow. He asked a shepherd, “Hey young man, what do you call this animal?” “Donkey!” said the boy.

The businessman bought the donkey and took him to Guizhou. The donkey had never seen a place like this before. He had always lived through either hot sultry summers or heavy rains. This was something new to him. He was very happy.

Guizhou was a beautiful place at the foothills of the mighty snow-capped mountains.

Lush green fields smiled at the bright sun. Cool, gentle breeze swayed the long, flat blades of grass that giggle and sing at the change of seasons. Squirrels ran around in glee. The donkey was delighted to see the place.

All day, the donkey ate green leaves and grass to his fill. He spent his time playing with rabbits and squirrels and grazing merrily. The businessman, however, had cautioned him, “You don’t have to work here, just spend your time the way you want. But make sure you are back home before the sun sets.”

Back in India,
the donkey had
to work hard all day.
He never got a chance
to enjoy his life. Here,
he was very happy.

The donkey always returned to his master in time. But one day, he got so engrossed in playfully chasing a squirrel that he forgot his master's warning.

A big burly tiger lived nearby. That very day, the tiger came out for his evening walk. When he saw the donkey for the first time he was taken aback. “I have never seen such an animal before. He must be some evil power, or how come his ears are so long and legs so thin?” thought the tiger. “I must stay away from him. I don’t want to be his supper!”

The tiger gave up his evening walk and hurried back to his den.

Though the tiger decided to stay away, he was very curious about the strange animal. Every morning, when the donkey came out to graze, the tiger would watch him from a hidden place.

After a few days, the tiger thought, "All the animals in my kingdom are afraid of me. I must see what this animal does when he sees me."

The next day when the donkey came to graze, the tiger slowly walked up to him. The donkey had seen tigers in India. He froze in fear. He gave out a loud cry, "Hee-haw, hee-haw." The tiger, on the other hand, was scared to hear such a strange call. And he fled at once.

Seeing the tiger running away, the donkey thought, "O, it's so much fun! Even a tiger here is afraid of a donkey like me."

He told all this to his master. The businessman said, “Never ever shall you go to the area again. The tiger will eat you up.” But the donkey paid no heed.

A few days later, the tiger gathered more courage and came to take an even closer look at the donkey. The tiger thought, “Whoever he may be, I am a tiger after all.”

When the tiger came really close, the donkey started kicking the tiger hard with his hooves.

For the tiger it was a gentle massage.
He enjoyed the donkey's kicks for a while.

"Oh, so this is all that you can do?" laughed the tiger, feeling relaxed. "What a fool I had been to think that you are more powerful than me!" he said.

And in a moment a beastly idea flashed across the tiger's mind. "I have tasted this animal's power, now let me taste its flesh," he said with a smile that spread out to his soft and fluffy ears.

He sprang upon the donkey and caught him by the neck. The donkey gave out a desperate cry, "Hee-haw, hee-haw!" But this could not frighten the tiger any more.

The tiger threw a deadly punch with its huge paw. This almost killed the donkey and stopped its bray. Then the tiger bit him to pieces and ate him with great relish.

FABULOUS FACT

A donkey's call (called 'bray') can be heard from more than three kilometres away.